DATE			

■ Science Experiments for Young People ■

Environmental Experiments About WATER

Thomas R. Rybolt

and

Robert C. Mebane

ENSLOW PUBLISHERS, INC.

Bloy St. and Ramsey Ave.
Box 777
Hillside, NJ 07205
U.S.A.

P.O. Box 38
Aldershot
Hants GU12 6BP
U.K.

For my daughter, Megan, with love. — TR

For my brother, Eddie. — RM

Library of Congress Cataloging-in-Publication Data

Rybolt, Thomas R.
Environmental experiments about water/ Thomas R. Rybolt and Robert C. Mebane.
p. cm. — (Science experiments for young people)
Includes index.
Summary: Presents experiments that focus on the properties of water, its cycle in nature, pollution problems, and methods of purification.
ISBN 0-89490-410-8
1. Water—Pollution—Experiments—Juvenile literature. 2. Water—Purification—Experiments—Juvenile literature. 3. Water—Experiments—Juvenile literature. [1. Water—Experiments. 2. Water—Pollution—Experiments. 3. Water—Purification—Experiments. 4. Acid Rain—Experiments. 5. Experiments.]
I. Mebane, Robert C. II. Title. III. Series.
TD422.R93 1993
628.1'68'078—dc20 92-41235
CIP
AC

Printed in the United States of America

10 9 8 7 6 5 4 3 2

Illustration Credit: Kimberly Austin

Cover Illustration: © Greg Vaughn/Tom Stack and Associates

CONTENTS

series contents for SCIENCE EXPERIMENTS FOR YOUNG PEOPLE

Introduction

Earth

Earth, our home in space, has supported life for billions of years. But with a growing human population, people are having a greater effect on the environment than ever before. Together we must learn about the problems facing our environment and work to protect the earth.

There are many ways we can work together to protect the earth. We can ask adults to use more fuel-efficient cars (cars that get more miles per gallon of gasoline). We can ride bikes or walk instead of getting rides in cars. We can recycle aluminum, paper, plastic, and glass, and we can plant trees. We can save energy by turning off lights when they are not in use. We can save energy by not keeping rooms and buildings too hot in the winter or too cold in the summer. Another way we can help the earth is to learn more about the environment.

This series of environmental books is designed to help you better understand our environment by doing experiments with air, water, land, and life. Each book is divided into chapters on topics of environmental concern or importance. There is a brief introduction to each chapter followed by a group of experiments related to the chapter topic. This series of environmental experiment books is intended to be used and not just read. It is your guide to doing, observing, and thinking about your environment.

By understanding our environment, we can learn to protect the earth and to use our natural resources wisely for generations to come.

Atoms and Molecules

Understanding something about atoms and molecules will help you understand our environment. Everything in the world around us is made of atoms and molecules. Atoms are the basic building blocks of all things. There are about 100 different kinds of atoms. Molecules are combinations of tightly bound atoms. For example, a water molecule is a combination of two hydrogen atoms and one oxygen atom.

Molecules that are made of only a few atoms are very small. Just one drop of water contains about two million quadrillion (2,000,000,000,000,000,000,000) water molecules.

Polymers are large molecules that may contain millions of atoms. Important natural polymers include natural rubber, starch, and DNA. Some important artificial polymers are nylon, which is used to make fabrics, polyethylene, which is used to make plastic bags and plastic bottles, and polystyrene, which is used in making styrofoam cups and insulation.

Atoms are made of smaller particles called electrons, protons, and neutrons. The nucleus is the center of the atom and contains protons and neutrons. Protons are positively charged, and neutrons have no charge. Electrons are negatively charged and surround the nucleus and give the atom its size.

Atoms and molecules that are charged are called ions. Ions have either a positive charge or a negative charge. Positive ions have more protons than electrons. Negative ions have more electrons than protons. Sodium chloride, which is the chemical name for table salt, is made of positive sodium ions and negative chlorine ions.

Atoms, ions, and molecules can combine in chemical reactions to make new substances. Chemical reactions can change one substance into another or break one substance down into smaller parts made of molecules, atoms, or ions.

Science and Experiments

One way to learn more about the environment and science is to do experiments. Science experiments provide a way of asking questions and finding answers. The results that come from experiments and observations increase our knowledge and improve our understanding of the world around us.

Science will never have all the answers because there are always new questions to ask. However, science is the most important way we gather new knowledge about our world.

This series of environmental experiment books is a collection of experiments that you can do at home or at school. As you read about science and do experiments, you will learn more about our planet and its environment.

Not every experiment you do will work the way you expect every time. Something may be different in the experiment when you do it. Repeat the experiment if it gives an unexpected result and think about what may be different.

Not all of the experiments in this book give immediate results. Some experiments in this book will take time to see observable results. Some of the experiments in this book may take a shorter time than that suggested in the experiment. Some experiments may take a longer time than suggested.

Each experiment is divided into five parts: (1) materials, (2) procedure, (3) observations, (4) discussion, and (5) other things to try. The materials are what you need to do the experiment. The procedure is what you do. The observations are what you see. The discussion explains what your observations tell you about the environment. The other things to try are additional questions and experiments.

Safety Note

Make Sure You:

- Obtain an adult's permission before you do these experiments and activities.
- Get an adult to watch you when you do an experiment. They enjoy seeing experiments too.
- Follow the specific directions given for each experiment.
- Clean up after each experiment.

Note to Teachers, Parents, and Other Adults

Science is not merely a collection of facts, but a way of thinking. As a teacher, parent, or adult friend, you can play a key role in maintaining and encouraging a young person's interest in science and the surrounding world. As you do environmental experiments with a young person, you may find your own curiosity being expanded. Experiments are one way to learn more about the air, water, land, and life upon which we all depend.

I. Properties of Water

Water is essential for life on earth. Two-thirds of the earth's surface is covered with water, but most of this water cannot easily be used by humans. Of the earth's water, 97 percent is salt water. The remaining 3 percent is either frozen at the poles, found underground, or found on the surface of the earth. Only 1 percent of the earth's water is found in rivers, streams, lakes, and marshes.

Often the water is not where it is most needed or the quality may be poor. The spreading of deserts, the loss of wetlands, the cutting of trees in rain forests, high levels of industrial pollution, and growing populations affect both the availability and the quality of water. Disease and illness in many developing countries are in part due to a lack of clean drinking water and a lack of treatment for water contaminated with waste and sewage.

Water is sometimes called the universal solvent because so many different substances will dissolve in it. These substances are often salts, like sodium chloride, that are made of ions that can separate into positive and negative parts. Smaller amounts of organic molecules, such as pesticides and pollutants, can also dissolve in water.

Water quality depends on many different properties, including acidity or alkalinity, temperature, color, odor, suspended solids, dissolved chemicals, dissolved gases (such as oxygen and carbon dioxide), and the presence of microorganisms (such as bacteria or protozoa).

Water in our environment is never found in a completely pure form. Even rainwater contains dissolved gases and chemicals that affect its properties. We study water and its properties to learn how to clean contaminated or polluted water, how to protect water from pollution, and how other substances and conditions affect water in the environment. This chapter includes experiments to study water acidity and density.

Experiment #1

Can You Measure the Acidity of Water?

Materials

- Red cabbage leaves
- Bowl
- Large jar with lid
- Measuring cup
- Measuring spoons
- Pen
- Pickling lime (available in grocery stores)
- Hot water
- Six clear, plastic cups
- White vinegar
- Baking soda
- Paper

Procedure

ASK AN ADULT TO HELP YOU WITH THIS EXPERIMENT. DO NOT GET ANY OF THE PICKLING LIME ON YOUR SKIN OR IN YOUR EYES. PICKLING LIME CAN HARM YOUR EYES AND IRRITATE YOUR SKIN. DO NOT DRINK ANY OF THE WATER WITH LIME IN IT.

Tear the red cabbage leaves into small pieces about the size of your thumb. Fill a bowl with the pieces of red cabbage. Cover the pieces of cabbage with hot water from a sink faucet. Wait about twenty minutes, and you should see the water turn purple. Pour the purple water into a large jar for use in this experiment. If your water supply is more basic (not neutral or acidic), the water may be blue.

You can save extra cabbage juice for future experiments. You can store the extra cabbage juice in a closed jar in a refrigerator so it will keep longer. You also can use this cabbage juice in experiments 6 and 8.

Add one-half cup of water to each of six clear, clean, plastic cups (glass jars or drinking glasses can be used instead). Add one-quarter cup of purple cabbage juice to each cup.

Place a piece of paper in front of each cup. Label one piece of paper "A." Label the next piece of paper "B." Continue until each piece of paper has one letter on it—A, B, C, D, E, or F. Place the papers in alphabetical order from left to right.

For the last part of this experiment, make sure your measuring spoons are clean and dry prior to each measurement. You will now begin to change the water to make it more acidic or more basic by adding other chemicals to the cups of water. The water in cup A will become the most acidic, and the water in cup F will become the most basic.

Add four teaspoons of vinegar to cup A. Add one-eighth teaspoon of vinegar to cup B. Do not add anything to cup C. Add a tiny pinch (amount you can hold between thumb and finger) of baking soda to cup D.

Add one-half teaspoon of baking soda to cup E. Add one teaspoon of pickling lime to cup F.

Observations

Look at each cup and write down the colors you see.

Discussion

To understand environmental problems involving water, we need to understand more about water itself. Water is a colorless liquid made of molecules. Each molecule of water has two hydrogen atoms bonded or connected to an oxygen atom. Using this chemical formula, water is written as H_2O.

One of the most important properties of water is how acidic or basic it is. An acid is something that adds a positive hydrogen ion (H^+) to water. A base is something that adds a negative hydroxide ion (OH^-) to water.

You cannot look at water and tell if it is acid, neutral, or base. However, there are molecules that change color as the acidity is changed.

Molecules that change color when mixed with an acid or base are called indicators. Cabbage juice contains indicators. In very acidic water, cabbage juice is red. In very basic (alkaline) water, cabbage juice is green. In slightly acidic water, cabbage juice is purple. In neutral to slightly alkaline water, cabbage juice is blue. A solution that is not acidic or alkaline is neutral.

Your results may be slightly different than what is discussed here. You can try changing slightly the amounts of vinegar, baking soda, or pickling lime you add to see if this makes a difference in the colors you observe. However, we expect the water in cup A to be red, cup B to be pink, cup C to be purple, cup D to be blue, cup E to be bluish-green, and cup F to be green.

The colors you observe indicate the acidity and alkalinity range of the water in the cups.

There is a scale used to measure acidity. It is called the pH scale. The pH scale has numbers that commonly range from 0 to 14. The most acidic value on the scale is 0. The most basic or alkaline value on the scale is 14. Water that is neutral, neither acidic nor basic has a value of 7. A decrease of one unit in the pH scale indicates a ten-fold increase in acidity.

There are many different types of acids and bases that can produce different pH values. Lemon juice has a pH of 2.0. Vinegar has a pH of 2.2. Milk has a pH of 6.6. Pure water has a pH of 7. Baking soda in water can give a pH of 8.2. Ammonia used for cleaning has a pH of 12.0. Natural rainwater without pollutants is slightly acidic with a normal pH of about 5.6. The acidity of most healthy lakes is above 6.

The acidity or alkalinity of natural water is affected by carbon dioxide gas found in the air. Carbon dioxide dissolves in water and naturally makes it slightly acidic. Carbon dioxide and water form a weak acid called carbonic acid. The pH of water determines what kinds of plants and animals can live in the water. Water that becomes too acidic or alkaline will kill plants and animals that live in the water.

Other Things to Try

You can test the acidity of water or other liquids by observing the color after adding cabbage juice. Try collecting some rainwater and testing its acidity. Add one-quarter cup of cabbage juice to one-half cup of water. Usually rainwater is only slightly acidic and should be purple with cabbage juice. What color does tap water give? What color do colorless, carbonated soft drinks give? Can you explain the colors you observe?

Try mixing different amounts of acidic and basic water and see what color changes you observe. Can you use this experiment to show that acids and bases can be combined to form neutral water?

Experiment #2

Can Temperature Change the Density of Water?

Materials

Sink
Water
Blue food coloring
Small plastic bottle with cap (pint size; 473 milliliters works well)

Procedure

Fill a sink with cold tap water. Add twenty drops of blue food coloring to a small, clean empty plastic bottle. Add hot water from the tap to the plastic bottle. After the bottle is completely filled with water, put the cap securely on the bottle. Shake the bottle to make sure the food coloring is spread throughout the water in the bottle.

Hold the sealed plastic bottle sideways on the bottom of the sink filled with water. While holding the bottle underwater, open the screw cap. The warm blue water should begin to come out of the bottle.

Observations

Watch the blue water. Does the warm, blue water spread

out into the colder, colorless water in the sink? Does the blue water settle to the bottom of the sink? Does the blue water rise? Does the blue water form a layer at the top of the sink of water?

Discussion

Water is a unique substance with many special properties. Solid water or ice is less dense than liquid water, and so ice floats on water. This is important because ice freezes on the top of lakes in the winter while the bottom stays a liquid.

Density is a measure of the mass of a certain volume. For example, oil has a lower density than water, so oil

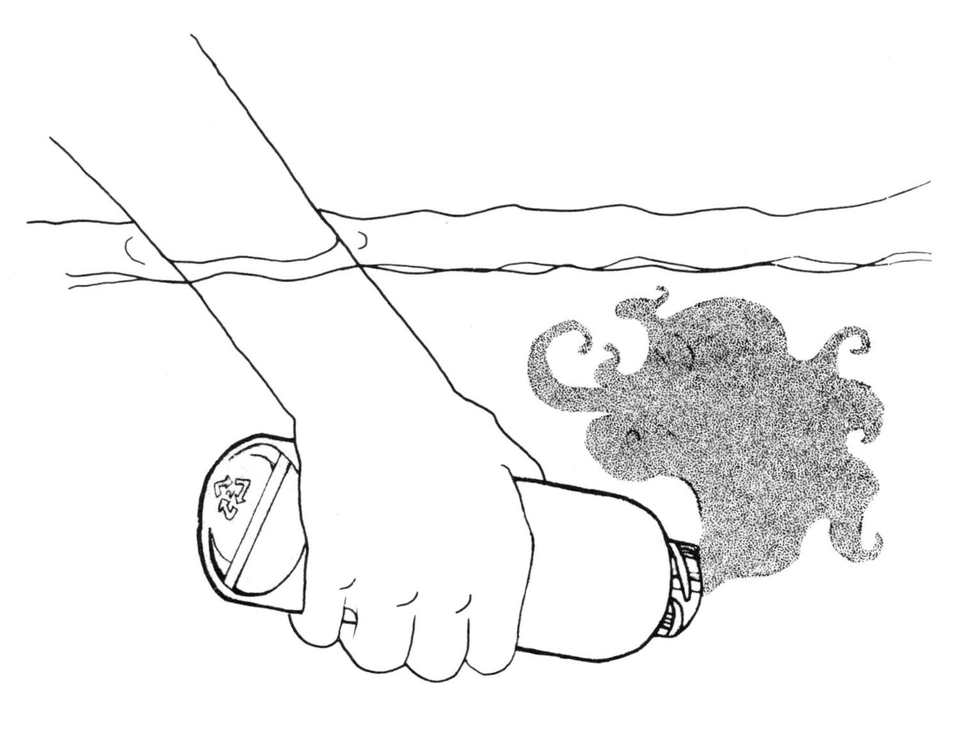

floats on top of water. The same volume of oil weighs less than the same volume of water.

The same volume of water can have a different weight if the density is changed. The density of water can change with temperature. The warm, blue water rises to the top of the sink filled with cold water because warm water has a lower density than cold water. You should see the blue water form a layer near the top of the sink of water. Both solid ice and hot water are less dense than cold water. Hot water is less dense because the molecules are farther apart. Solid ice is less dense because the molecules lock into positions that hold them farther apart than in cold water.

The effect of temperature on the density of water is important in the environment of lakes and rivers. Often water from lakes and rivers are used for cooling in power plants and industrial plants. After use in the plant, the water is returned to the lake or river from which it was taken. This would not cause a problem except that the returned water is warmer.

Returning warmer water to a lake or river causes thermal pollution. The warmer or hot water can hold less air and has a lower density than the naturally colder water. The lower density hot water floats on top of the colder water and prevents air from going into the cold water. This is most serious in deep lakes. The warm water on top keeps oxygen from the air from reaching fish and other aquatic life deeper in the lake.

One solution to the problem of thermal pollution is to cool the water partially before it is returned to lakes or rivers. Often power plants and industrial plants have large cooling towers which are used to cool hot water and thus decrease thermal pollution.

Other Things to Try

Try this experiment with different colors of food coloring. Does the color of the water make any difference?

Try this experiment with the hot and cold water switched. Fill the sink with hot tap water, but not so hot you cannot put your hands into the water. Add twenty drops of food coloring to the bottle and fill the bottle with cold tap water. Put the cap securely on the bottle. Shake the bottle to make sure the food coloring is spread throughout the water in the bottle.

Hold the sealed plastic bottle sideways on the bottom of the sink filled with water. While holding the bottle underwater, open the screw cap. What happens to the cold, blue water as it comes out into the warm sink water? Does the cold water go to the top or settle on the bottom? Does this agree with what you expect?

II. Water Cycle

The water cycle, or hydrologic cycle, is the movement of water from the ocean to the air to the land and back to the ocean again. The cycle of water in nature involves evaporation, condensation, and precipitation. The evaporation of water, primarily from the ocean, changes the water from a liquid to a vapor or gas. Condensation is the collection of vapor into droplets or ice crystals in the upper atmosphere. Precipitation is the falling of a liquid, such as rain, or solids, such as hail, sleet, or snow, back to the earth.

Although most of the precipitation falling on land comes originally from seawater, the actions we take on land can still affect the water cycle. Converting forest to pasture land, draining swamps, paving roads, building shopping malls, and increasing demands for water can affect the water cycle and may reduce the amount of water in underground aquifers or natural storage areas.

The fresh water that humans use comes from surface water and groundwater. Surface water is found in lakes, rivers, and streams and may be frozen as ice or snow. Groundwater goes through soil and cracks in rock to fill in the available spaces between sand and rocks. The surface of the groundwater is called the water table. This may drop if water is pumped out of the ground faster than it can be refilled by nature. Groundwater can also be harmed by gasoline leaking from storage tanks, fertilizers, waste from sewers and septic tanks, and other pollutants.

The water cycle is nature's way of providing us with a supply of clean water, but we must use available water wisely. In this chapter, we will do experiments to learn more about the water cycle, changing liquids to solids, and evaporation.

Experiment #3

How Can You Demonstrate the Water Cycle?

Materials

Water
Ice
Stove
Two metal saucepans
Insulated glove (such as oven mitt)

Procedure

ASK AN ADULT TO HELP WITH THIS EXPERIMENT. DO NOT USE THE STOVE BY YOURSELF. If one of the two pans is larger, select this pan. Fill this pan half full with water. Heat this pan of water on a stove until it is boiling.

Fill the second pan with ice. Have an adult use an insulated glove to carefully hold the pan filled with ice about ten inches above the pan of boiling water. DO NOT LET THE STEAM FROM THE BOILING WATER TOUCH YOUR SKIN. STEAM IS HOT AND CAN BURN.

Watch the space between the two pans for several minutes. When you are finished, be sure to turn off the stove.

Observations

Do you see a cloud rising into the air from the hot water? What happens to the steam leaving the boiling water? Do you see drops of water form on the bottom of the cold pan? Do these drops of water become larger and fall back into the boiling water?

Discussion

Some of the water in the pan on the stove leaves as steam or water vapor. This hot steam rises in the air and strikes the bottom of the cold pan. When the molecules of water in the steam hit a cold surface, some are cooled enough to change to liquid water. The liquid water on the bottom of the cold pan can form drops of water that fall back into the boiling water. This falling of liquid water completes the water cycle.

On a larger scale, there is a water cycle in nature called the hydrologic cycle that is similar to the water cycle you have demonstrated. The natural water cycle involves three main parts: evaporation, condensation, and precipitation. The hydrologic cycle helps purify water and provides our rain and snow.

The heat energy from the sun warms the earth and causes evaporation of water. In evaporation, liquid water is changed to a gas or vapor. As a gas, the molecules of water vapor are spread throughout the air and cannot be seen. Water vapor is invisible. Water vapor comes from all bodies of water on the earth, including oceans, lakes, ponds, rivers, and marshes. Water vapor is also given off by plants in a process called transpiration. In transpiration, plants give off moisture through the surface of leaves. Water vapor rises into the air with warm air.

When warm moist air rises, it meets cooler air higher in the atmosphere and begins to change from a gas back to a liquid. The change from a gas to a liquid is called condensation. Initially, the liquid water is formed in very small droplets. These droplets form around particles of dust in the atmosphere. These tiny droplets of liquid water scatter light that is passing through them and appear white. These tiny water droplets form clouds high in the atmosphere or fog near the surface of the earth.

The white cloud you see above boiling water is not the steam but droplets of liquid water condensed from the hot steam. In this experiment, some steam condenses in the cooler air, and more condenses on the bottom of the cold pan.

Clouds in the atmosphere are made of tiny water droplets. When these droplets combine to form water drops, they may fall as rain. If the temperature is cold enough, the water may form solid ice and fall to the ground as snow or hail. Or ice may melt and form drops of water as it falls. Rain, snow, sleet, and hail are forms of precipitation.

Precipitation may go directly back to the ocean or to the land. Precipitation on the land may go into surface water, such as lakes, rivers, or streams, or into underground water. Also, precipitation may go into the soil to be used by plants.

In your experiment, water was evaporated from the pan of hot water. Then some water condensed in the cooler air, and more condensed on the bottom of the cold pan. The condensed drops grew larger. Some of these large drops on the bottom of the cold pan fell like precipitation back to the hot water where they started.

Other Things to Try

Repeat this experiment and try varying the distance between the pan of ice water and the boiling water. How does raising the pan affect the amount of water condensing on the bottom of the pan?

Try boiling a mixture of salt water. Does the water that collects on the bottom of the cold pan taste salty? You should find that salt does not evaporate with the water. This is important because it means that fresh, pure rainwater can come from the ocean as well as from lakes and rivers.

Try this experiment outside. Hit a chalk eraser to make a cloud of dust and then spray water from a hose over this dust. Does this show how the hydrologic cycle can help clean dust and pollution from the air?

Experiment #4

Can Water Vapor From the Air Change Directly to Solid Ice?

Materials

Water
Ice
Table salt
A tablespoon
A large drinking glass
Measuring cup

Procedure

Fill the glass half full with ice cubes. Add six tablespoons of salt to the ice and stir to mix the ice and salt together. Add a few more ice cubes to the glass and then pour about one-quarter cup of water into the glass. Feel the sides of the glass. Look at the outside of the glass.

Stir the salt and ice in the glass a few times every minute. Continue to stir the mixture approximately every minute while the glass stands on the table or counter. After about ten minutes, feel the sides of the glass. Look at the outside of the glass. If there has been no change, continue to stir the salt ice mixture and observe the outside of the glass. You may need to add more ice cubes to the glass.

Observations

Is the outside of the glass dry at the beginning of the experiment? After you have stirred the ice and salt for several minutes, does water freeze on the outside of the glass?

Discussion

You should find that the outside of the glass is dry when you start the experiment. However, as time goes on, water vapor from the air freezes on the outside of the cold glass.

A mixture of salt and ice has a temperature lower than 0° C (32° F)—the freezing point of water. A mixture of salt and ice can have a temperature as low as -22° C (-8° F). Salt changes the melting process of ice so that a salt and water mixture can stay a liquid below 0° C.

We cannot see water vapor in the air. Water vapor in the air exists as individual water molecules. Humidity is a measure of the amount of water vapor in the air relative to the maximum amount possible. Humidity changes with season and place. The humidity is lower in the winter when the air is cold and dry.

Molecules of water that strike the side of the cold glass can change from a gas to a solid. As time passes, more water molecules, which are always moving in the air, freeze on the outside of the glass. You can see the frost and feel the frozen water on the outside of the glass.

To replenish our water supplies, warm moist air rising from the earth meets colder air and forms droplets of water or ice crystals. Water molecules cluster together on small solid particles of dust or smoke or salt. It may take millions of these tiny droplets to form one rain drop. The droplets

come together to form larger drops that then fall as rain. Snow may fall in the cold, upper atmosphere and then melt to rain before it reaches the earth.

Over much of the earth's surface, the upper atmosphere is cold enough so that the droplets form ice crystals. These ice crystals may grow larger and then fall to the earth. If the temperature near the earth is warm enough, the ice melts and falls as drops of rain. If the temperature is cold near the surface, the ice crystals remain and fall as snow. If the temperature is warm and then cold going toward the earth, the ice may melt and then refreeze and fall as sleet. If the ice particles are carried up and down in the upper atmosphere, the ice crystals may grow to large hailstones and fall as hail.

Other Things to Try

Repeat this experiment using only ice and water in the glass but no salt. Since the temperature of ice and water is not as cold, you should find that only water forms on the outside of the glass. Condensed water is like dew on grass. Frozen water is like frost. Frost only forms in the winter when the air and ground are much colder.

Use a thermometer and measure the temperature of a mixture of ice and water. Use a thermometer and measure the temperature of a mixture of ice, salt, and water. Check the temperature of a refrigerator and the temperature of a freezer. Can ice stay as a solid in the refrigerator?

Experiment #5

How Does Heat Energy From the Sun Affect Water on the Earth?

Materials

Water
Paper towels
Watch
Two plates

Procedure

You should do this experiment on a warm, sunny day. Pour enough water on each paper towel to make a wet spot about the size of your fist. Place one paper towel on a plate inside your house or apartment out of the sun. Place the second paper towel on a plate and set the plate outside in the sunshine. You may need to place something on the paper towel so the wind does not blow it away.

Touch the center of each paper towel once every five minutes. Continue this for at least thirty minutes.

Observations

Are both paper towels wet at the beginning of the experiment? Are both paper towels wet every time you touch them? Does one paper towel dry out first?

Discussion

You should find that the paper towel placed in the sun will

dry out before the one left inside. Given a long enough time, the wet paper towel left inside may also dry out.

What happened to the water in the paper towel that was placed in the sunshine? The water left the towel and went into the air. This change of water from a liquid to a gas is called evaporation.

The heat energy from the sun causes water to evaporate. When water evaporates, liquid is changed to a gas or vapor. As a gas, the molecules of water vapor are spread throughout the air and cannot be seen. Water vapor comes from water on the earth and from water in the soil. Water vapor is also given off by plants in a process called transpiration. In transpiration, plants

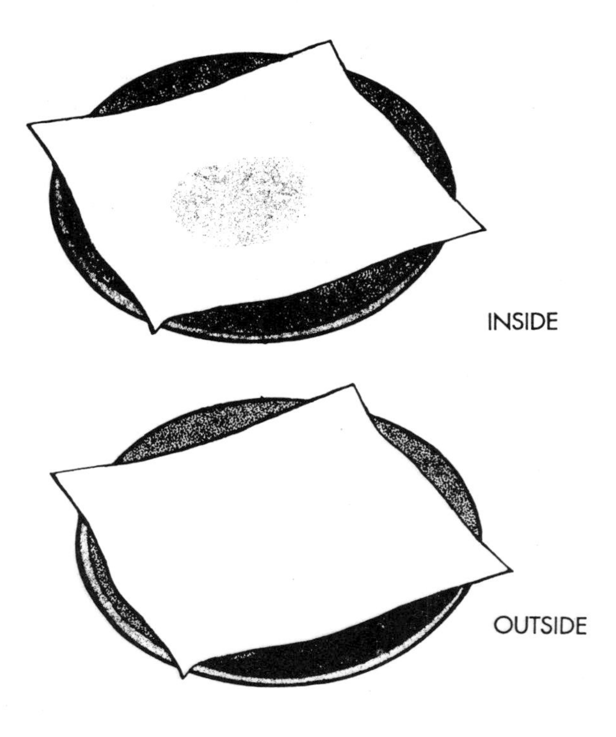

give off moisture through the surface of leaves. Water vapor spreads throughout the air.

Evapotranspiration is the combined evaporation from bodies of water and from soil and transpiration from plants. Low humidity, or little water in the air, and high temperatures tend to increase the amount of evapotranspiration. Windy conditions also tend to increase evaporation.

Enough water is evaporated every year to cover the entire surface of the earth with a layer of water one meter (about 39 inches) deep. Evaporated water stays in the air about ten days before falling back to earth as precipitation such as rain or snow.

Most of the water carried into the atmosphere by evaporation comes from the ocean. About six times as much evaporated water comes from the ocean as from land water and moisture given off by plants. However, about four times as much precipitation falls on the seas as the land. So the land surface is gaining extra water that comes from the ocean. Some of this extra land water returns to the ocean through rivers. In general, 90 percent of all the precipitation that falls on the land is from water that comes from the ocean. However, in rain forests, much more of the rain comes directly from water evaporated from the rain forest.

Outdoor watering causes almost a one-third increase in water use in the United States during the summer. If you live in a place where the lawn or plants are watered, you can use what you have learned about evaporation to save water. Water from sprinklers can evaporate five times faster during the hot midday than in the cooler morning. Watering in the morning can save water. Watering in the evening can also save water but may cause fungus to grow in the grass, so morning is probably a better choice.

Other Things to Try

Wet the bottom half of two paper towels. Tape the dry portion of one paper towel to a table so the wet half hangs down toward the floor. Ask an adult to set an electric fan so the air blows directly on this paper towel. Tape the second paper towel in a place where it can hang without the air from the fan blowing on it. Check each paper towel for wetness once every five minutes. Does this show that blowing air also helps water evaporate?

Fill a clear glass measuring cup with enough water to bring the level to the two-cup mark. The cup may also have metric measurements on the side. (One cup is the same as 237 milliliters.) Place the measuring cup on a piece of aluminum foil outside where the sun will shine directly on the cup. Write down the exact level of the water. Check the water level again each hour for at least four hours. Does the water level drop? Where is the water going? Can you explain what causes the water to leave the cup?

III. Acid Rain

It is normal for rain, snow, lakes, and rivers to be slightly acidic because carbon dioxide in the atmosphere combines with water to form carbonic acid in rain. However, there has been a great increase in the burning of fossil fuels such as coal, oil, and gasoline to produce energy for factories and homes and to power our vehicles of transportation. Sulfur dioxide and nitrogen oxides can be produced during the burning of fossil fuels and are the pollutants responsible for the problem of acid rain. Burning these fossil fuels has made rainwater more acidic.

Acid rain wears down building materials made of marble, limestone, and sandstone. Acid rain may also affect the lime used in cement or mortar that holds bricks and concrete blocks together. Acid rain can also increase the corrosion on metal surfaces such as on cars, steel bridges, and copper statues. Corrosion wears away the surface, causes cracks, and can shorten the useful lifetime of many metal objects.

Rain falling on some parts of North America is 10 to 100 times more acidic than natural. This acid rain can cause trees in forests to die and can kill plants and animals in lakes and ponds.

We need to work on ways to reduce sulfur dioxide

and nitrogen oxide emissions from power plants and automobiles so that our environment and living things are not harmed by increasing amounts of acid rain. In this chapter, you will do experiments that look at the causes, effects, and treatments of acid rain.

Experiment #6

Can Carbon Dioxide Cause Water to Become More Acidic?

Materials

Red cabbage leaves
Bowl
Large jar with lid
Bottle of carbonated (seltzer) water
Measuring spoons
Hot water
Measuring cup

Procedure

If you have saved cabbage juice from experiment 1, you can use it and skip the first part of this procedure.

If you do not have any cabbage juice from experiment 1, then do the following. Tear the red cabbage leaves into small pieces about the size of your thumb. Fill a bowl with the pieces of red cabbage. Cover the pieces of cabbage with hot water from a sink faucet. Wait about twenty minutes, and you should see the water turn purple. Pour the purple water into a large jar for use in this experiment. If your water supply is not acidic but more basic, the water may be blue.

You can save extra cabbage juice for future experiments. You can store the extra cabbage juice in a closed jar in a refrigerator so it will keep longer. You also can use this cabbage juice in experiment 8.

Add one cup of carbonated water to a clear glass. Add one cup of water from a faucet to another clear glass. Add one-fourth cup of cabbage juice to the carbonated water. Add one-fourth cup of cabbage juice to the regular tap water.

Observations

Look at each cup. What colors do you see in each?

Discussion

Molecules that change color in an acid and base are called indicators. Cabbage juice contains indicators. In very acidic water, cabbage juice is red. In very basic water, cabbage juice is green. In slightly acidic water, cabbage juice is purple. In neutral to slightly basic water, cabbage juice is blue. A liquid that is neither acidic nor basic is neutral.

Carbonated water sold in bottled drinks has extra carbon dioxide added to it. We see the extra carbon dioxide gas bubble out when we open the bottle. However the extra carbon dioxide gas shows us how gases in the air can cause water to become more acidic. Carbon dioxide combines with water to make carbonic acid.

Bottled carbonated water has enough carbonic acid to cause cabbage juice to turn red. Lakes and rivers have some carbonic acid but not as much as in a carbonated drink, so regular water would normally be purple when cabbage juice is added.

Carbon dioxide gas combines with water to form carbonic acid. Since there is always carbon dioxide present in the air, it is normal for lakes and rivers to be slightly acidic because of carbonic and other natural acids. Do you see how other gases in the air could cause rainwater and snow to become even more acidic? The main gases that have caused an unnatural increase in acidity are sulfur dioxide, which comes from burning coal, and nitrogen oxides, which come from high temperature engines.

Electronic meters called pH meters are used to measure the exact acidity or alkalinity of water. These meters use a scale called pH that varies from 0 to 14. On this scale 0 is extremely acidic, 14 is extremely basic or alkaline, and 7 is neutral. As the numbers get smaller, the water gets more acidic. Each decrease of one unit indicates a ten-fold increase in acidity. So a pH value of 4 is ten times as acidic as a pH of 5, a hundred times as acidic as a pH of 6, and one thousand times as acidic as a pH of 7.

Normal rainwater has a pH of about 5.6, and the acidity of most healthy lakes is above 6. A pH below 4.5 is low enough to kill all the fish in a lake.

Other Things to Try

You can test the acidity of water or other liquids by observing the color after adding cabbage juice. Try collecting some rainwater and testing its acidity. Add one-quarter cup of cabbage juice to one-half cup of water. Usually, rainwater is only slightly acidic and should be purple with cabbage juice. Test lemon juice and see what color the cabbage juice turns.

Add the minimum amount of baking soda to adjust the water and cabbage juice to a faint blue color. Put a straw in the water and blow through the straw. You may have to blow for twenty minutes or more to see a change.

See if the carbon dioxide from your breath will cause the water to change color from blue to purple.

Add a small amount of baking soda to adjust the water and cabbage juice to a blue color. Try leaving some of this blue cabbage juice in a jar open to the air for several days. See if enough carbon dioxide from the air will dissolve in the water to turn it back to a purple color.

Experiment #7

Can Acid Rain Damage Buildings and Statues?

Materials

- Vinegar
- Small bowl
- Two pieces of chalk
- Water
- Clear glass

Procedure

Some types of chalk work better than others for this experiment. You may have to try several kinds to find one made of calcium carbonate that should work for this activity. Some dustless chalk does not work well because of how the chalk has been treated.

Place one piece of chalk in the glass. Add enough water to the glass to completely cover the chalk. Place the second piece of chalk in the bowl. Add enough vinegar to the bowl to completely cover the chalk. Watch the pieces of chalk for several minutes.

Leave the pieces of chalk in the bowl and glass overnight. The next morning take the pieces of chalk out of the water and out of the vinegar. Compare the two pieces of chalk.

Observations

Do you see bubbles of gas in the glass when the chalk is placed in water? Do you see bubbles of gas in the bowl when the chalk is placed in vinegar? Where are the bubbles coming from?

After the pieces of chalk have remained in the vinegar and water overnight, how are they different?

Discussion

There are many different types of acids. Lemon juice and vinegar are common acids. Vinegar is a mixture of acetic acid and water. Food acids like vinegar and lemon juice have a sour taste. You should never taste an unknown acid since some acids are harmful.

Some brands of chalk are made of a mineral called limestone. Another name for limestone is calcium carbonate. Limestone is sometimes used to make buildings. Limestone has been used for many years to make statues. Some Greek statues that are thousands of years old are made of limestone.

When acid gets on limestone, the calcium carbonate is broken apart. Calcium ions and carbon dioxide gas are two of the things that are formed. The bubbles you see in the bowl with the vinegar are carbon dioxide. The bubbles form on the surface of the chalk. The chalk in the vinegar gets smaller because the acetic acid in the vinegar breaks the calcium carbonate in the chalk apart.

Acid rain can hurt statues and buildings in the same way.

Marble, limestone, and some kinds of sandstone are building materials that are all made of large amounts of calcium carbonate. Sulfuric acid from acid rain can react with calcium carbonate to make calcium sulfate or gypsum. Gypsum is soft and dissolves in water. As gypsum is washed off the surface, part of the stone surface is carried away.

Acid rain may also affect the lime used in cement or mortar that holds bricks and concrete blocks together. Lime is a white solid of calcium oxide used in making mortar and cement. An acid attack on the mortar or the stone surface can cause cracks and weaken the wall or surface.

Acid rain can also increase the corrosion on metal surfaces, such as on cars, steel bridges, and copper statues. Corrosion wears away the surface, causes cracks, and can shorten the useful lifetime of many metal objects.

Normal rainwater is slightly acidic because carbon dioxide in the air dissolves in water. However, in some parts of the world, there is more acid in the rain than normal. This type of rain is called acid rain. Acid rain not only harms plants and animals but can also damage materials like stone and metal.

Scientists believe that acid rain is caused by sulfur dioxide and nitrogen oxides. Sulfur dioxide is a type of air pollution produced by burning fuels that contain sulfur atoms. Sulfur dioxide in the air is changed to sulfur trioxide. When sulfur trioxide gets in rainwater, it produces sulfuric acid. Sulfuric acid is one cause of acid rain. Nitrogen oxides are another type of pollution that causes acid rain. Nitrogen oxides in the atmosphere can form nitric acid in rain and ice.

Other Things to Try

Repeat this experiment using carbonated water from a colorless soft drink such as Sprite. Does the carbon dioxide gas in the soft drink make the water acidic enough to break down chalk? Cover a piece of chalk with lemon or grapefruit juice. Watch the bubbles of carbon dioxide that form. Pour out the juice and pour water over the chalk. Do the bubbles stop? The bubbles will stop if there is no acid on the chalk.

Cover a piece of chalk in a bowl with water. Add vinegar until bubbles first begin to form. How much vinegar did you add to the water? Try the same thing with lemon juice. How much lemon juice did you add until bubbles began to form? Which is more acidic, vinegar or lemon juice?

Some antacid tablets contain calcium carbonate. Place a few drops of lemon juice on top of an antacid tablet. Do you see bubbles of carbon dioxide? Wait a few minutes and feel the surface of the tablet. Do you feel a soft surface that tends to flake off?

Experiment #8

Can Liming Help Protect Lakes From Acid Rain?

Materials

Red cabbage leaves	Bowl
Measuring spoons	Hot water
Large jar with lid	Jar
Measuring cup	Vinegar
Pen	Paper

Pickling lime (available in grocery stores)

Procedure

ASK AN ADULT TO HELP YOU WITH THIS EXPERIMENT. DO NOT GET ANY OF THE PICKLING LIME ON YOUR SKIN OR IN YOUR EYES. PICKLING LIME CAN HARM YOUR EYES AND IRRITATE YOUR SKIN. DO NOT DRINK ANY OF THE WATER WITH LIME IN IT.

If you have saved cabbage juice from experiment 1 or 6, you can use it and skip the first part of this procedure.

If you do not have any cabbage juice from experiment 1 or 6, then do the following. Tear the red cabbage leaves into small pieces about the size of your thumb.

Fill a bowl with the pieces of red cabbage. Cover the pieces of cabbage with hot water from a sink faucet. Wait about twenty minutes, and you should see the water turn purple. Pour the purple water into a large jar for use in this experiment.

You can save extra cabbage juice for future experiments. You can store the extra cabbage juice in a closed jar in a refrigerator so it will keep longer.

Add one-half cup of water to a clear jar. Add one-quarter cup of cabbage juice to this jar of water. Add two tablespoons of vinegar to this jar. The purple cabbage juice should now be red.

Add exactly one-fourth teaspoon of lime to the red water. Add an additional one-fourth teaspoon of lime to this water. Again, add one-fourth teaspoon of lime to the water. As you add the lime, if you observe no change, you might try swirling the jar to help the lime mix with the water more quickly.

Observations

Each time you add lime to the water write down the color you observe.

Discussion

Cabbage juice contains molecules called indicators that change color depending on the acidity of the water. Indicators are different colors in acid and base. In very acidic water, cabbage juice is red. In very basic water, cabbage juice is green. In slightly acidic water, cabbage juice is purple. In neutral and slightly basic water, cabbage juice is blue. A solution that is not acidic or basic is neutral.

An acid is something that makes a positive hydrogen ion (H^+) in water. A base is something that makes a negative hydroxide ion (OH^-) in water. A hydrogen ion is a hydrogen atom with an electron removed. A hydroxide ion is a hydrogen and oxygen atom with an extra electron.

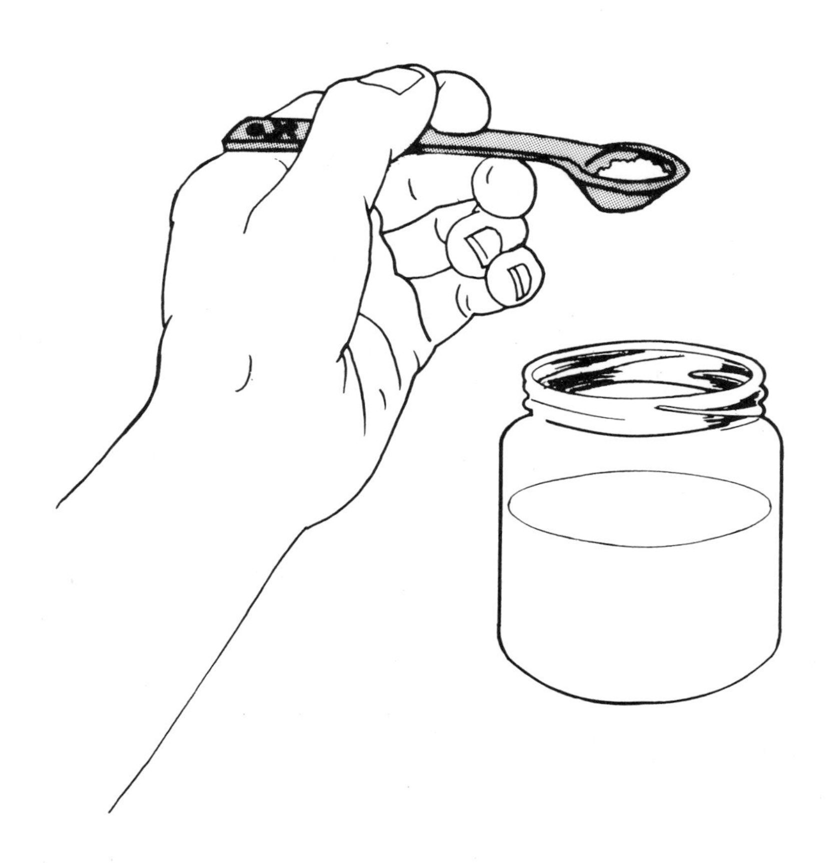

We expect the vinegar and cabbage juice mixture to be red at the beginning of the experiment because vinegar is an acid. As you add lime, we expect to see color changes because lime is a base. As lime is added, the acidity of the water decreases.

You may see the color change from red to purple to blue to green with each one-fourth teaspoon of lime added. Your results may be slightly different from what is discussed here. You can try changing slightly the amounts of lime you add to see if this makes a difference in the colors you observe.

Lime is made of a chemical called calcium oxide. As you have seen in this experiment, lime can be used to make acidic water become more neutral or basic.

Lime or limestone are sometimes added to lakes and ponds to make them less acidic. Lime is a strong base. Limestone that contains calcium carbonate is a weaker base. Adding lime to a lake is called liming. The lime can be added to a lake by pouring it out of a boat or dropping it out of an airplane.

Liming can keep ponds and lakes from becoming more acidic. It does not cure the problem of acid rain, but it can keep the lake from becoming so acidic that plants and fish die. Liming has to be repeated every few years, but it has been used successfully in the United States, Canada, and Scandinavian countries. Liming may help us control the acidity of lakes while we seek to control the sources of acid rain.

Other Things to Try

Repeat this experiment using baking soda (sodium bicarbonate) or baking powder (partly sodium carbonate) instead of lime. Are bubbles of carbon dioxide given off when these are added? Does it take more baking soda or lime to neutralize acidic water?

Can you add enough baking soda to the purple cabbage water to make it turn green? You should find that you can only get the water to turn blue using baking soda. Which is more basic, lime or baking soda?

You can test other substances to see if they can neutralize acid. Does table salt (sodium chloride) or Epsom salt (magnesium sulfate) have any effect on acidity?

Try adding one tablespoon of lime to a cup of purple cabbage juice. The lime should turn the water green. Now try adding vinegar one tablespoon at a time to the green water. Write down the color after each tablespoon of vinegar is added. Some of the lime does not dissolve in the water. This extra lime keeps the water from turning acid until extra vinegar is added.

IV. Water Pollution

Through natural processes such as erosion and decay, all water contains dissolved or suspended substances. Some natural substances found in water include gases such as air, salts, organic material from plants and animals, microorganisms such as bacteria, and solids such as sand and clay. Water quality is a measure of the types and amounts of these substances in the water.

Water quality is also affected by people. In addition to the natural contaminants found in water, many pollutants are being added to our water supplies by human activities. Major sources of water pollution are sewage, industrial wastes, and the runoff of agricultural fertilizers and pesticides. Other sources of water pollution include oil spills, seepage from landfills, septic tanks, mines, and underground fuel storage tanks. Water pollution also can be caused by storm-water runoff from streets, parking lots, and buildings and even the dumping of household chemicals down the drain.

Water pollution lowers water quality and presents a potential health problem. In addition, water pollution destroys the natural beauty and health of lakes, rivers, and oceans. In the experiments that follow, you will learn more about water pollution, how it affects our environment, ways to control it, and ways to avoid it.

Experiment #9

What Happens When Too Many Nutrients Are Added to Lakes and Ponds?

Materials

- Pond water
- Plant fertilizer
- Measuring spoons
- Two clear, one-half-gallon glass jars with lids
- Tape
- Felt pen

Procedure

ASK AN ADULT TO HELP YOU FILL EACH GLASS JAR WITH WATER FROM A POND OR LAKE. IF YOU GO NEAR THE EDGE OF A POND OR LAKE, HAVE AN ADULT WITH YOU.

Place a piece of tape on each jar. Use the felt pen to label one jar "fertilizer" and the other jar "no fertilizer."

You will need to use a fertilizer that readily dissolves in water. Most fertilizers for indoor plants will dissolve in water and will work well. Also, you will need to choose a fertilizer that is high in nitrogen and phosphorus. Most fertilizers have three numbers listed on their labels. Use a fertilizer that has a large first and second number. A large first number means the fertilizer contains a large amount of nitrate and a large second number means the fertilizer contains a large amount of phosphate. For instance, the label might say 20-20-20.

Add two tablespoons of fertilizer to the jar labeled "fertilizer." Secure a lid on the jar and shake the jar to dissolve the fertilizer.

Remove the lids from both jars and place them outdoors where they will get plenty of sun. Observe the jars every day for a month.

Observations

What color is your pond water? Is your pond water cloudy? Do you see things floating in the pond water? What color is your plant fertilizer? What color is the pond water after you add the plant fertilizer? Does the pond water containing the plant fertilizer turn cloudy after a week or two? Does the pond water containing the plant fertilizer eventually turn green?

Can you see algae growing in the pond water containing the plant fertilizer? If you see algae in the pond water containing the plant fertilizer, is there algae growing in the pond water that does not contain plant fertilizer?

Discussion

A healthy pond, lake, or river contains clear, fresh water that includes a plentiful amount of oxygen that is dissolved in the water. Dissolved oxygen is essential for fish and other aquatic life and to the overall health of the body of water.

In healthy bodies of water, dissolved oxygen is constantly used and produced. Fish and other aquatic life use the oxygen and release carbon dioxide and animal waste into the water. Animal waste is made of organic material.

Bacteria in the water use some of the dissolved oxygen in the water to decompose or break down the animal waste to nutrients. Bacteria also break down other organic material, such as dead plants and animals, into nutrients with the use of dissolved oxygen. Aquatic plants, such as algae, then use the carbon dioxide and

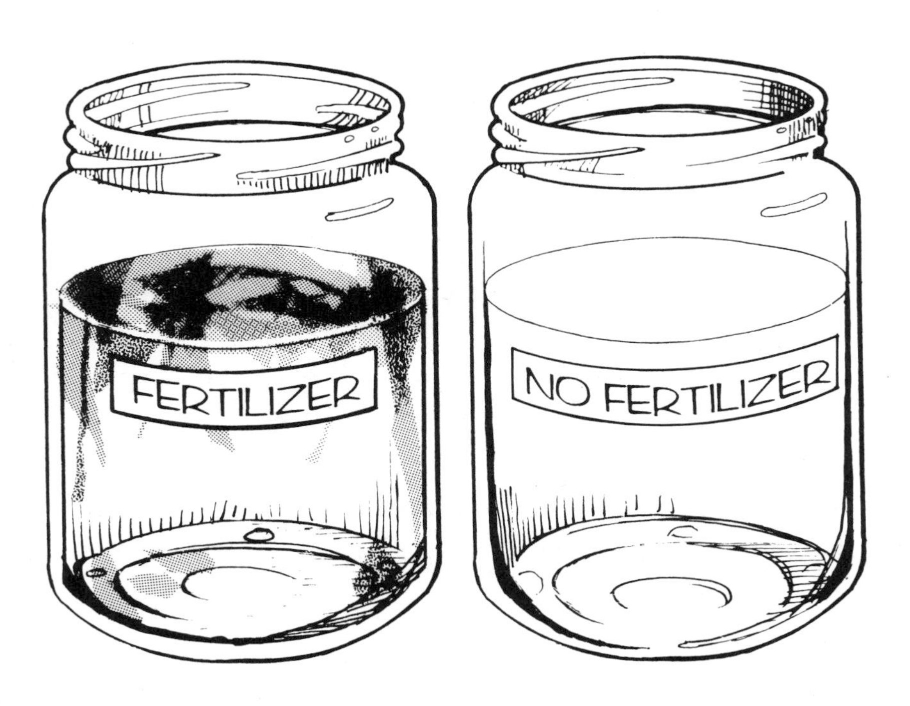

nutrients in the water and release oxygen back into the water.

There is a balance between the use and production of dissolved oxygen in healthy ponds, lakes, and rivers. If additional nutrients are added to a healthy pond, lake or river, the number of aquatic plants and animals increases. The body of water can become overcrowded with aquatic plants and animals. Organic material slowly accumulates from algae, bacteria, aquatic plants, and animal waste. Bacteria use the dissolved oxygen in the water faster than it is made. Less dissolved oxygen becomes available for aquatic life in the pond or lake. This process of using up dissolving oxygen is called eutrophication. Eutrophication can cause ponds and lakes to become choked with green, slimy algae and then become lifeless and stagnant.

The major nutrients that cause eutrophication are nitrates and phosphates. These nutrients can get into ponds, lakes, and rivers from runoff of fertilizers used on farms and lawns, from waste from cattle, and from wastewater from sewage plants.

In this experiment, you should observe that the pond water containing the plant fertilizer becomes green and cloudy after a week or two. The pond water that does not contain plant fertilizer should have little or no green color or cloudiness. The green cloudiness is due to rapidly growing algae. Algae grow rapidly in the pond water containing the plant fertilizer because there is an excess of nitrate and phosphate nutrients in the pond water.

After a month, you should see a green, slimy mass of algae in the pond water containing the plant fertilizer. You should also see some algae that has died and settled to the bottom of the jar. This is just like what happens in ponds, lakes, and rivers that are undergoing eutrophication.

Other Things to Try

Leave your jars containing pond water outdoors for several months. You may have to add water occasionally. What happens to the pond water in each jar after this time?

Repeat this experiment with water from a sink faucet. Do you get similar results?

Repeat this experiment with different amounts of plant fertilizer. What do you observe?

Ask a trusted adult to take you to several ponds and lakes in your area. A good time to go is in the summer. Look along the edge of the pond or lake. Do you see a lot of algae growing? If you do, then the pond or lake may have too many nutrients in it from agricultural or city wastewater runoff.

Experiment #10

Can the Pollutant Phosphate Be Removed From Water?

Materials

Water
Two tall, clear glasses
Plant food
Measuring cup
Alum (available in many grocery and drug stores)
Measuring spoons
Tape
Felt pen

Procedure

This experiment requires a source of aluminum ions. Alum is a good source and should be available in many grocery and drug stores. If you cannot find alum, carefully crush in a small plastic bag a piece of a styptic pencil (made from alum), which should be available in most drugstores. You can also use aluminum sulfate, which can be found in the fertilizer section of many hardware stores.

Put a piece of tape on each glass. Label one glass "fertilizer" and the other "alum" with the felt pen.

Add one-quarter cup of water to each glass. Add one teaspoon of alum to the glass labeled "alum" and stir with a spoon for thirty seconds. Some of the alum may not dissolve. Allow the alum water to sit for one minute.

Add one tablespoon of plant food to the glass labeled "fertilizer" and stir with a spoon to dissolve the fertilizer in the water. Choose a fertilizer that dissolves easily in water and that is high in phosphorus. Most fertilizers have three numbers listed on their labels. Use a fertilizer that has a large second number. This means the fertilizer contains a large amount of phosphorus in the form of phosphate. This experiment was tested with plant food that was labeled 20-20-20.

Add one teaspoon of the alum water to the glass labeled "fertilizer" and make your observations. Observe the contents of the glass after it has set undisturbed for two hours.

To clean up, pour the alum water down the drain and rinse the glass thoroughly with water. The fertilizer water can be added to one gallon of water and used to water plants.

Observations

What color is the alum? Does all of the alum dissolve in the water? Is the alum water clear?

What color is the fertilizer? Does all of the fertilizer dissolve in the water? Is the fertilizer water clear?

Do you see a cloudy solid form in the glass labeled "fertilizer" when you add one teaspoon of the alum water to the glass?

Discussion

Phosphates are important plant nutrients and are used in most fertilizers. In some areas of the country, phosphates are also used in detergents to increase the cleaning power of the detergents.

Runoff of fertilizers from farmland when it rains and the release of wastewater containing phosphates can cause phosphates to end up in ponds and lakes. Since phosphates are a plant nutrient, this could cause eutrophication of the ponds and lakes. Eutrophication is the process in which excess plant nutrients in ponds and lakes cause algae and other aquatic plants to grow so

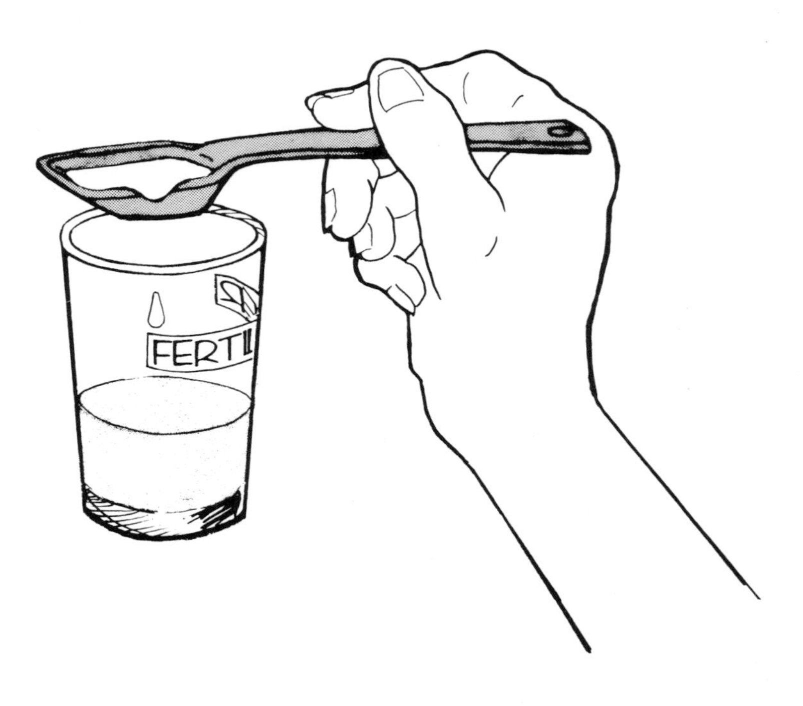

rapidly that the water becomes choked with aquatic plants.

Because phosphates can lead to eutrophication, many areas of the country have banned or restricted the use of detergents with a high phosphate content. Also, some cities have advanced wastewater treatment plants that remove phosphates from city wastewater before the treated water is released into rivers or lakes. Advanced wastewater treatment plants remove the phosphate from water with aluminum ions.

Alum is a name used for salts that contain aluminum sulfate. A common alum is potassium aluminum sulfate. Potassium aluminum sulfate is a salt made of potassium ions, aluminum ions, and sulfate ions. When this alum dissolves in water, the potassium, aluminum, and sulfate ions break apart from each other and become surrounded by water molecules.

When you add alum water to the fertilizer water, you should see a cloudy solid appear. The aluminum ions in the alum water combine with phosphate ions in the fertilizer water to form a new chemical substance called aluminum phosphate. Aluminum phosphate is not soluble in water. This is why a cloudy solid appears. This cloudy solid is called a precipitate. You should observe that the aluminum phosphate precipitate slowly settles to the bottom of the glass.

Nitrates are another major plant nutrient that can cause eutrophication of ponds and lakes. Nitrates, like phosphates, can get into ponds and lakes from fertilizer runoff, from city wastewater, and from farm animal wastes.

Besides being a cause of eutrophication, nitrates can be a health problem if drinking water becomes contaminated with them. Drinking water with too many nitrates in it can cause the blood to carry less oxygen. This health problem is called methemoglobinemia and is particularly dangerous for infants.

Nitrates are more difficult to remove from water than phosphates. Expensive and complex equipment is required, and most communities with advanced wastewater treatment plants do not have this equipment.

Other Things to Try

Repeat this experiment using just one teaspoon of fertilizer. Do you get as much precipitate?

Repeat this experiment with a plant fertilizer containing little or no phosphates. A fertilizer containing no phosphates will have a zero listed as the second number of the three-number label on the fertilizer. What do you observe?

Experiment #11

What Is Thermal Water Pollution?

Materials

Water
A small saucepan
A stove
A cooking thermometer (optional)

Procedure

ASK AN ADULT TO HELP YOU WITH THIS EXPERIMENT. DO NOT USE THE STOVE BY YOURSELF.

Fill a small saucepan half full with cold water from a sink faucet. If you have a cooking thermometer, place it in the pan of water (a cooking thermometer is optional and is not necessary for this experiment). Heat the saucepan on the stove using medium heat. Closely watch the bottom and the sides of the saucepan for tiny air bubbles. If you placed a cooking thermometer in the water, note the temperature of the water when you first see air bubbles appear on the bottom and the sides of the saucepan.

Continue to heat the saucepan to boil the water. Boil the water for two minutes. Turn off the stove and allow the water to cool for fifteen minutes.

Reheat the saucepan of water on the stove using

medium heat. Closely watch the bottom and the sides of the saucepan for tiny air bubbles. Turn off the stove when the water starts to boil. TO KEEP FROM POSSIBLY BURNING YOURSELF, ALLOW THE HOT WATER IN THE SAUCEPAN TO COOL BEFORE YOU POUR IT INTO A SINK.

Observations

Do you see any air bubbles under the water sticking to the bottom or sides of the saucepan before you start heating? Do you see wavy lines in the water when you first start to heat the water? Do you see tiny bubbles form on the bottom and the sides of the saucepan after a few seconds of heating? If you placed a cooking thermometer in the saucepan, what is the temperature of the water when you first see tiny bubbles appear in the water? Do the bubbles get larger as you continue to heat? Do some of the bubbles break away from the bottom and sides of the saucepan and float to the surface of the water?

Do you see any air bubbles on the bottom or the sides of the saucepan of water after it has been boiled for two minutes and then cooled for fifteen minutes? Do you see wavy lines in this water when you first start reheating the water? Do you see any tiny bubbles form in the water as you heat the water to boiling?

Discussion

Soon after you begin heating the water on the stove, you should start to see tiny bubbles forming under the water and sticking to the bottom and sides of the saucepan. These tiny bubbles contain air. The air in these bubbles was dissolved in the water before you started heating the water. The wavy lines you see in the water are convection currents. Convection currents are caused by different temperatures in the water.

Air, which is a gas, can dissolve in water just like table salt and sugar, which are solids. However, unlike table salt and sugar, only a small amount of air will dissolve in water.

Less air dissolves in warm and hot water than in cold water. Air dissolved in water will form bubbles when the water is heated. The bubbles can escape the water by floating to the surface of the water.

If you placed a cooking thermometer in the saucepan of water, you should have noticed that the tiny air bubbles formed in the water at a temperature around 40° C (104° F). Water normally boils at a temperature of 100° C (212° F). Water changes to a gas when it boils. Most of the bubbles you see in boiling water are water that has changed to a gas.

As you continued to heat the water, the bubbles of air sticking to the bottom and sides of the saucepan should have become larger. A gas expands or takes up more space as it is heated. You may have seen some bubbles become large enough to break away from the bottom or sides of the saucepan and float to the top of the water.

You should have noticed that few, if any, bubbles formed in the water that was reheated after it was boiled for two minutes and allowed to cool for fifteen minutes. This is because all of the dissolved air was removed from the water when it was boiled for two minutes.

Water from lakes and rivers is used by some industries for cooling purposes. The major industrial users of water from lakes and rivers for cooling are power plants that use steam to generate electricity. Metal, plastic, chemical, and petroleum producers also use water from lakes and rivers for cooling purposes.

When water is used to cool things, the water becomes warm. This warm water contains less dissolved air. If this warm water is returned directly to a lake or river, then there will be less dissolved air in the water. This means there will be less dissolved oxygen available for aquatic life. Fish must breathe faster in warmer water because there is less oxygen in the water. Fish may have to leave the area, or they may even die.

When warm water is returned to lakes and rivers by industries, this is called thermal pollution.

Warm water is also less dense than colder water. This means warmer water will float on colder water. This can be harmful to aquatic life that lives in the deeper parts of lakes because the warm water floating on the surface keeps oxygen from dissolving and reaching lower depths of lakes.

Other Things to Try

Repeat this experiment using hot water from a sink faucet. Do you see as many air bubbles when you first start to heat the hot water?

Boil some water in a saucepan for two minutes and allow the water to sit undisturbed for twenty-four hours. Reheat the water to boiling. Does air redissolve in the undisturbed water?

Experiment #12

Can Oil Be Soaked Up From Oil Spills?

Materials

- Water
- Toothpicks
- Bubble gum
- Refrigerator-freezer
- A hand-held food grater
- A piece of paper
- Disposable aluminum pie pan
- Household machine oil (such as 3-IN-ONE)

Procedure

Place a piece of bubble gum in the freezer section of the refrigerator-freezer and leave it there overnight. You will want to use a hard piece of bubble gum instead of the soft variety. Also, use bubble gum that is packaged as a chunk instead of a stick. It is easier to grate the chunk-style bubble gum. This experiment was tested with Super Bubble brand of bubble gum.

Fill the pie pan about half full with water. Carefully drip ten drops of household machine oil on the surface of the water. Try to drip the oil drops on top of each other to form one large drop of oil floating on the surface of the water. You can use a toothpick to gather small drops of oil into one large drop if necessary.

Remove the bubble gum from the freezer and remove the wrapper surrounding the gum. Place the hand-held food grater on a piece of paper. ASK AN ADULT TO GRATE THE BUBBLE GUM USING THE MEDIUM GRATE ON A HAND-HELD FOOD GRATER. TELL THEM TO BE CAREFUL AND NOT TO SCRAPE THEIR FINGERS. The adult should grate about one-fourth of the piece of bubble gum onto the piece of paper. Most of the grated gum should look like tiny strings while some will look like small particles about the size of sand.

Carefully tilt the piece of paper over the oil drop and sprinkle the grated bubble gum over the entire oil drop. Also, sprinkle some of the grated gum in the water.

Use the toothpick to move the gum-covered oil around. Push the gum-covered oil drop under water with the toothpick. Try picking up some of the gum-covered oil drop with two toothpicks. Observe the gum-covered oil after it has remained undisturbed in the water for thirty minutes.

Observations

Does the oil float or sink on the pan of water? What happens when the grated gum is added to the oil drop? Does the grated gum dissolve in the water? Can you pick up the gum-covered oil with two toothpicks? Is the oil still mixed with the gum after the thirty minutes?

Discussion

Oil, or petroleum, is an extremely valuable natural resource because it is a major source of energy. Petroleum is used mostly as fuel for industry, heating, and transportation. Petroleum is also an important source of raw materials for the manufacture of a number of materials such as plastics, synthetic fibers, insecticides, detergents, paints, and some medicines.

Oil spills, either on land or water, can be harmful to the environment. Oil spilled on the ground can contaminate groundwater, streams, rivers, and lakes that may be used as sources of drinking water. Oil spills on water can be harmful to aquatic plants, fish, and other animals that live in or around the water.

Some of the more dramatic oil spills have occurred in the oceans and seas of the world. The largest spill to date is thought to be the dumping by Iraq in the Persian Gulf of an estimated ten million barrels of crude oil during the Persian Gulf War in 1991. The largest oil spill in the United States to date occurred when over a quarter million barrels of crude oil spilled off Alaska's coast on March 24, 1989, when the oil tanker *Exxon Valdez* struck a reef.

Several techniques can be used to clean up oil spills on water. One technique involves surrounding the spill with a floating fence called a boom and using pumps and skimmers to remove the oil from the surface of the water. Another technique uses dispersants, which are special detergents. When the dispersants are sprayed on oil spills, the oil breaks up into tiny droplets that mix with the water.

Two other ways developed to clean up oil spills include using oil-absorbing materials that act like a sponge and soak up the oil or burning the oil on the surface of the water.

Recently, special oil-eating bacteria have been developed that may be used in the future. By far the best way to deal with an oil spill is the prevention of spills in the first place.

In this experiment, you learn how gum in bubble gum can be used to soak up oil on the surface of water. Bubble gum is a mixture of gum base, sugars, colors, and flavors. Gum base is made of polymer molecules. Polymer molecules are made of thousands of smaller molecules. The smaller molecules are connected together to make long polymer molecules.

The polymer in bubble gum is not soluble in water. This means it does not dissolve in water. It does not dissolve in water because water is polar and the gum polymer is nonpolar. In general, like dissolves like. For example, sugar dissolves in water because both sugar and water are polar. Grease dissolves in gasoline because both grease and gasoline are nonpolar. Oil does not dissolve in water because oil is nonpolar and water is polar. Also, since oil is lighter than water, oil floats on water.

You should notice that the grated bubble gum mixes with and soaks up or absorbs the oil drop on the surface of the water. The gum and oil mix together because both of these materials are nonpolar. Even after thirty minutes, the oil and gum should remain mixed.

A material containing an ingredient similar to the gum in chewing and bubble gum has been developed for soaking up oil spills at sea. The material is spread over the oil spill as a fine powder so that it will rapidly dissolve in the oil spill. The material makes the oil in the spill stick together so that it can be removed from the surface of the water as a sheet by either a pump or a skimmer.

Other Things to Try

Repeat this experiment with different types of chewing and bubble gums. Do all gums work? Try this experiment using different types of oils.

V. Water Purification

Earth is referred to as the water planet because nearly 80 percent of the earth's surface is covered by water. Most of this water is seawater found in the ocean. Only 3 percent of the water on earth is fresh water, and most of this fresh water is frozen in glaciers as ice.

The amount of water on earth does not change. There is the same amount of water on earth today as there was millions of years ago.

Nearly all of the water to be used for drinking and other human needs must be treated to make it safe. In the United States, over thirty-four billion gallons of water are treated each day by water treatment plants. These treatment plants purify water by removing suspended particles, bacteria, and substances that produce color, taste, and odor in the water.

Most of the water on earth is seawater and is unfit for drinking, irrigation, and industrial uses because it contains large amounts of dissolved salts. However, as the population of the world continues to increase and as the demand for fresh water continues to increase, the removal of salts from seawater to make fresh water is becoming increasingly more important. In the following experiments, you will learn more about purifying water and making fresh water from seawater.

Experiment #13

How Is Drinking Water Purified?

Materials

- Four glass jars
- Water
- Soil
- Small paper cup
- Household ammonia
- Coffee filter
- Alum (available in many grocery and drug stores)
- Clean sand (available at most hardware stores)
- Measuring cups
- Measuring spoons
- A sharpened pencil
- Tape
- Felt pen

Procedure

DO NOT DRINK WATER FROM ANY OF THE JARS IN THIS EXPERIMENT.

Place a piece of tape on each glass jar. Use the felt pen to label the jars "cloudy," "alum water," "treated," and "filtered." Make sure to write on the tape.

If you live in a sandy area, you may want to use potting soil or topsoil, which is available in many stores, for this experiment. Place one tablespoon of soil into the jar labeled "cloudy." Add one cup of water from a sink faucet to this jar. Stir the soil and the water with a spoon for fifteen seconds. Allow the water in the jar to settle for one hour.

To make alum water, pour one cup water from a sink faucet into the jar labeled "alum water." Add one teaspoon of alum and stir to dissolve the alum in the water.

Carefully pour the cloudy, dirty water from the jar labeled "cloudy" into the jar labeled "treated." Avoid transferring any of the dirt that has settled on the bottom of the jar. Add one tablespoon of the alum water from jar "alum water" to the cloudy, dirty water in the jar "treated."

ASK AN ADULT TO USE A SPOON TO CAREFULLY ADD FIVE DROPS OF HOUSEHOLD AMMONIA TO THE CLOUDY WATER IN JAR LABELED "TREATED." DO NOT GET AMMONIA ON YOUR SKIN OR IN YOUR EYES. Stir with a spoon. If you do not see a fine solid form, add five more drops of ammonia and stir again. Allow this water to settle for one hour.

Use the sharpened end of the pencil to punch a hole slightly larger than the size of the pencil lead into the bottom of a small paper cup. Use your fingers to push the coffee filter into the paper cup. The coffee filter should completely line the inside of the paper cup.

Carefully fill the lined paper cup three-fourths full with clean sand. While holding the paper cup containing the sand over the jar labeled "filtered," slowly pour the water from the jar labeled "treated" over the sand. Make sure to collect the water coming from the bottom of the paper cup into the jar labeled "filtered." DO NOT DRINK THE FILTERED WATER BECAUSE IT HAS

NOT BEEN DISINFECTED AND MAY CONTAIN BACTERIA OR OTHER MICROORGANISMS THAT COULD MAKE YOU SICK.

The unused alum water should be rinsed down the sink with water. The jar labeled "cloudy" should be rinsed outside with water to remove any dirt in it.

Observations

Does the water in the jar labeled "cloudy" become less cloudy as the water in the jar settles for one hour?

After the alum water and ammonia have been added to the cloudy water, do you see a milky solid that looks like tiny pieces of cotton in the water? Does this milky solid settle to the bottom of the jar after one hour? Is the water above the settled, milky solid clear?

Does the sand filter trap the settled milky solid? Is the water dripping from the paper cup containing the sand clear?

Discussion

Water for drinking and other human needs is purified in several steps. The water to be purified is first pumped from a source of water to the treatment plant. The source of water could be either surface water or groundwater. Surface water comes from streams, rivers, ponds, lakes, or reservoirs. Groundwater comes from wells or natural springs.

If surface water is the source of water to be treated,

it first passes through screens to remove debris such as logs, sticks, fish, and plants. Groundwater usually does not contain debris because it is filtered by the ground.

Next, chemicals are mixed with the water that aid in the removal of small suspended particles in the water. These chemicals are called flocculents.

Most water companies use the chemical aluminum sulfate, or chemicals made from aluminum sulfate, as a flocculent. When aluminum sulfate is added to the water, it is changed into the chemical aluminum hydroxide by natural substances in the water that are basic. Basic substances neutralize substances that are acids. Sometimes the water company has to add chemical substances that are basic to the water to change the aluminum sulfate into aluminum hydroxide.

The aluminum hydroxide that forms in the water is a gelatinlike solid that absorbs and entangles small suspended particles in the water. The combination of the aluminum hydroxide and trapped suspended particles is called a floc. Some bacteria become trapped in the floc, also.

For the next step, the treated water slowly flows through a settling basin to allow most of the floc to settle to the bottom of the basin. Then the water is filtered through gravel and sand to remove the last traces of floc. Some water companies filter their water through charcoal to remove substances in the water that are colored or have an odor. In a final step, a disinfectant, such as chlorine or ozone, is added to the water to kill any remaining bacteria.

In this experiment, you remove suspended particles from water similar to the way a water treatment plant does. You should notice that even after settling for one hour, the water you mixed with dirt still appears cloudy. This cloudy appearance of the water is called turbidity, and the water is said to be turbid. Turbid water has small suspended particles in it. One measure of water quality is the turbidity of the water.

When the alum water and ammonia are added and stirred in the water, you should see the formation of a solid that looks like tiny pieces of cotton. This solid is the gelatinlike aluminum hydroxide that forms the floc with the suspended particles in the water. The floc should settle to the bottom of the jar after about an hour. The water above the settled floc should be much less turbid. When you filter the water, you should notice that the floc is trapped by the sand and that the water dripping from the paper cup is clear of suspended particles.

Other Things to Try

To learn how the water in your area is purified, visit your local water treatment plant. Most water treatment plants welcome visitors. Not all people get their drinking water from treatment plants. Some people get their water from wells. Usually, well water is not treated because it has been naturally filtered.

ASK AN ADULT TO HELP YOU COLLECT SOME WATER FROM A POND OR LAKE. DO NOT GO NEAR THE EDGE OF A POND OR LAKE WITHOUT AN ADULT. Repeat this experiment with the pond or lake water. Does the water become clear after you treat it with alum and filter it through sand? DO NOT DRINK THE FILTERED WATER BECAUSE IT HAS NOT BEEN DISINFECTED AND MAY CONTAIN BACTERIA AND OTHER MICROORGANISMS THAT COULD MAKE YOU SICK.

Repeat this experiment with one cup of water from a sink faucet that has three drops of red food coloring added to it. Is the red color removed by this purification process?

Experiment #14

Can Organic Chemicals Be Removed From Water?

Materials

- A measuring cup
- A small paper cup
- A spoon
- A coffee filter
- Water
- A sharpened pencil
- Red food coloring
- Tape
- Three clear drinking glasses
- Activated carbon (used in fish aquarium filters)
- Felt pen

Procedure

Use the sharpened end of the pencil to punch a hole slightly larger than the size of the pencil lead into the bottom of a small paper cup. Place the coffee filter in the paper cup. Use your fingers to push the coffee filter into the paper cup. The coffee filter should completely line the paper cup.

Use a spoon to fill the lined paper cup three-fourths full with the activated carbon. Activated carbon (charcoal) can be found in pet stores and some large retail stores. Some brands of activated carbon may be more effective than others in this experiment.

Fill a measuring cup with one cup of water. Add one drop of red food coloring to the water. Stir the water and food coloring with a spoon until well mixed.

Put a piece of tape on each drinking glass. Use the felt pen to label the glasses "filter 1," "filter 2," and "colored water." Pour one-half cup of the colored water into the glass labeled "colored water."

While holding the paper cup containing the activated carbon over the glass labeled "filter 1," slowly pour the remaining one-half cup of colored water over the activated carbon. Make sure to collect the water coming from the bottom of the paper cup into the glass labeled "filter 1." Compare the color of the water dripping into the glass labeled "filter 1" with the water in the glass labeled "colored water."

Now hold the paper cup containing the activated carbon over the glass labeled "filter 2." Slowly pour the water in the glass labeled "filter 1" into the paper cup containing the activated carbon. Make sure to collect the water coming from the bottom of the paper cup into the glass labeled "filter 2." Compare the color of the water dripping into the glass labeled "filter 2" with the water in the glass labeled "colored water."

Observations

What color is the activated carbon? Is there less red color in the glass labeled "filter 1" than in the glass labeled "colored water?" Are there tiny black particles in the filtered water? Is there even less red color in the glass labeled "filter 2" than in the glass labeled "colored water?" Does the filtered water appear gray in color?

Discussion

Activated carbon is a special type of charcoal that can absorb chemicals that contain carbon atoms. Chemicals that contain carbon atoms are called organic chemicals.

When organic chemicals adsorb on activated carbon, they actually stick to the surface of the carbon. Each activated carbon particle has a large surface on which organic chemicals can stick. Although you cannot see

them, the pieces of activated carbon contain many cracks and crevices on their surfaces.

In this experiment, you use food coloring to show that activated carbon can remove organic chemicals from water. Food coloring molecules are made of carbon and other atoms. When you pour the red-colored water into the cup containing the activated carbon, you should see that the water coming out of the bottom of the cup has less red color than the water you poured onto the activated carbon. This is because most of the red food coloring molecules stick to the surface of the activated carbon. When you pass the water in the glass labeled "filter 1" through the activated carbon a second time, more red food-coloring molecules should be removed. If the water appears gray, then some extremely tiny carbon particles are passing through the coffee filter. You can try using several coffee filters together to keep the tiny carbon powders from going into the filtered water.

Many water companies use activated carbon to remove organic chemicals that may be present in their water sources. Also, some people use special activated carbon filters in their homes to clean water for drinking. Organic chemicals that could be found in water as pollutants include pesticides and herbicides from agricultural runoff, transportation fuels from leaking underground storage tanks, oils washed from streets and parking lots by rain, and solvents used by industries to clean materials. Organic chemicals can also be made by algae and certain bacteria found naturally in water.

Other Things to Try

Repeat this experiment using other food colors. Do you get similar results?

Repeat this experiment using five drops of red food coloring in a cup of water. How many passes through the activated carbon are necessary to remove most of the red color from the water?

How many times can you use the activated carbon to decolorize water before it is no longer effective at adsorbing food coloring?

Experiment #15

Can Water and Salt Be Separated From Seawater by Freezing?

Materials

- A tall drinking glass
- Measuring cups
- Water
- Table salt
- Measuring spoons
- Refrigerator-freezer
- Ice cubes
- A spoon

Procedure

Pour one cup of water into a tall drinking glass. Add one and one-half teaspoons of table salt to the water. Stir the water and table salt with a spoon until all the table salt disappears (dissolves). Taste the salt water by dipping a clean spoon first into the salt water and then on your tongue. DO NOT DRINK THE SALT WATER. Place the glass of salt water in the freezer section of the refrigerator-freezer.

Using a spoon, check the glass of salt water every thirty minutes for the formation of ice crystals. When you have enough ice crystals in the salt water to form a slush, you are ready for the next step described in the following paragraph. You do not want all of the salt water to freeze.

Fill a measuring cup with one cup of cold tap water from a sink faucet. Add several ice cubes to the cold tap water. Stir the ice cubes and water with a spoon for thirty seconds to make the tap water ice cold. You are going to use this ice cold tap water to wash the ice crystals that have formed in the slushy saltwater mixture in the freezer.

Remove the glass of slushy salt water from the freezer. Stir the slush with a spoon for ten seconds. Tilt this glass over a sink and carefully drain as much water from the glass as you can. Use the spoon to keep ice from sliding out of the glass as you drain the water.

Add one-quarter cup of the ice cold tap water to the ice crystals in the glass. Using a clean spoon, stir the water and ice crystals for five seconds. Tilt the glass over a sink and drain as much water from the glass as you can. Quickly wash and drain the ice crystals three more times with one-quarter cup of ice cold tap water.

Allow the washed ice crystals to melt. Taste the water by dipping a clean spoon first into the water and then on your tongue.

Observations

Can you taste the salt in the salt water you made for this experiment? How long does it take for ice crystals to form in the glass of salt water? Are the ice crystals big or small? Do some of your ice crystals melt when you wash them with ice cold tap water? Can you taste any salt in the water that formed when the washed ice crystals melted?

Discussion

In this experiment, you show that the salt and water in seawater can be separated by changing the water into ice. When water freezes, individual water molecules pack closely together in a tight pattern to form ice crystals. Pure water freezes at 0° C (32° F). Seawater freezes at a lower temperature of -3° C (27° F).

When sodium chloride is placed in water, it breaks into positive sodium ions and negative chlorine ions. These ions have a shape different than water molecules and do not pack easily next to solid water molecules on the growing ice crystals. The ions are pushed away from the growing ice crystals. However, if all the water freezes, then the ions will become trapped in the ice.

You may taste some salt in the water from the melted and washed ice crystals. This is because some salt ions do get trapped in the ice crystals. Also, your tongue is extremely sensitive to the taste of salt. However, the melted ice should be much less salty.

Other Things to Try

Repeat this experiment using different amounts of salt. Do you get similar results?

Can you remove more salt from the washed, melted water by refreezing it to make a slush? Try it and see.

Experiment #16

Can Water and Salt Be Separated From Seawater by the Sun?

Materials

Water
Table salt
Measuring cup
Measuring spoons
A dark-colored piece of paper
A small glass (a juice glass is a good size)
A clean, clear, large, wide-mouth glass jar with lid

Procedure

In this experiment you will need a small glass that will fit inside a large glass jar. A juice glass is a good size. Also, you will want to do this experiment on a sunny day.

Add one and one-half teaspoons of table salt to one cup of water and stir to dissolve the salt in the water. Taste the salt water by dipping a clean spoon first into the salt water and then on your tongue. DO NOT DRINK THE SALT WATER.

Set the clean, large glass jar outside in the sun on a dark-colored piece of paper. Choose a spot where it can stay for several hours in the direct sun.

Fill the small glass nearly three-fourths full with the salt water. Carefully place this glass of salt water inside the large glass jar. Avoid spilling any salt water in the large jar. Tighten the lid on the jar.

After three hours of sitting in the sun, remove the lid from the glass jar. Carefully lift out the glass containing the salt water. Dip a clean spoon in the water that is now inside the large jar. Taste the water on the spoon.

Observations

Can you taste the salt in the salt water you made for this experiment? Do drops of water appear on the side, top, and bottom of the large glass jar as it sits in the sun? How long does it take for water to appear on the sides of the glass jar? Can you taste any salt in the water that forms inside the glass jar?

Discussion

This experiment shows that fresh water can be made from salt water by a process called distillation. However, it is not possible for you to actually make seawater for this experiment because seawater contains many different salts. Instead, you are simulating seawater by dissolving table salt (sodium chloride) in water. The salt water you make in this experiment has about the same salinity as seawater. Salinity, also called salt content, is the amount of salt in seawater. The average salinity of seawater is around thirty-five grams of salts in each kilogram of water.

Distillation involves first changing a liquid into a gas or vapor. This is called evaporation and requires energy. Next, the vapor is cooled so that it can change back to a liquid. This change from a vapor to a liquid is called condensation.

In this experiment, you use energy from the sun to heat the salt water in the small glass. Some of the water in the glass changes from a liquid to a vapor. The vapor spreads into the jar and cools when it hits the side of the jar. When the vapor cools enough, it changes back to a liquid.

Energy from the sun evaporates water but not the salt. The salt remains in the glass. Even if all of the water in the glass is changed into a vapor and condenses on the inside surface of the jar, all of the table salt you originally added will remain in the small glass.

When energy from the sun is used to distill a liquid, the process is called solar distillation. Solar distillation is used in parts of the Middle East to make fresh water from seawater for human needs.

The process of making fresh water from seawater is called desalination. In addition to solar distillation, fresh water can be made from seawater by freezing and by osmosis. Freezing changes water to a solid but leaves the salt in the unfrozen liquid. When fresh water is made from seawater by osmosis the seawater is pumped through a material, called a membrane, that allows water to pass through it but does not allow salts to pass through it.

Other Things to Try

Can you make more fresh water by leaving the jar containing the glass of salt water in the sun for several days?

Repeat this experiment at night and on a cloudy day. Is the sun really necessary for this experiment to work well?

Repeat this experiment but add a drop of food coloring to the salt water. Are you able to purify this colored salt water by solar distillation?

Complete List of Materials Used in These Experiments

A
alum
ammonia, household

B
baking soda
bowl
bubble gum

C
carbon, activated
carbonated (seltzer) water
chalk
coffee filter
cup, small paper

F
food coloring, blue
food coloring, red
food grater, hand-held

G
glasses, clear
glass, large drinking
glass, small
glove, insulated

I
ice
ice cubes

J
jars, glass
jars, one-half gallon, glass with lids
jars, large with lid

M
machine oil, household
measuring cup
measuring spoons

P
paper
paper, dark-colored
paper towels
pen
pen, felt
pencil
pickling lime
pie pan, aluminum
plant fertilizer
plant food
plastic bottle, small with cap
plastic cups, clear
plates

R
red cabbage leaves
refrigerator-freezer

S
salt, table
saucepan, small
saucepans, metal
sink
soil
spoon
stove

T
tape
thermometer, cooking
toothpicks

V
vinegar, white

W
watch
water, hot tap
water, pond

Index